John Burningham

The Shopping Basket

RED FOX

Other books by John Burningham

Avocado Baby	Seasons	*Little Books*
Aldo	Time to get out of the Bath, Shirley	The Dog
Courtney	Come Away from the Water, Shirley	The School
ABC	Would You Rather?	The Friend
Cloudland	The Shopping Basket	The Baby
Granpa	Where's Julius?	The Cupboard
Trubloff	Oi! Get off our Train	The Snow
Humbert	Mr Gumpy's Outing	The Rabbit
Harquin	Mr Gumpy's Motor Car	The Blanket
Borka	John Patrick Norman McHennessy	
Simp		

A Red Fox Book

Published by Random House Children's Publishers UK
61-63 Uxbridge Road, London W5 5SA

A division of Random House UK Ltd
Addresses for companies within The Random House Group Limited
can be found at : www.randomhouse.co.uk/offices.htm

30 29 28 27 26 25

First published in Great Britain by Jonathan Cape Ltd 1980
Reprinted 1982, 1985, 1989, 1994, 1995, 2002

This Red Fox edition 2000

Printed in Singapore

RANDOM HOUSE UK Limited Reg. No. 954009

ISBN 978 0 099 89930 3

www.randomhousechildrens.co.uk

"Pop down to the shop for me, will you, Steven, and buy six eggs, five bananas, four apples, three oranges for the baby, two doughnuts and a packet of crisps for your tea. And leave this note at number 25."

So Steven set off for the shop, carrying his basket.
He passed number 25,

the gap in the railings,

the full litter basket,

the men digging up the pavement

and the house where the nasty dog lived,

and arrived at the shop.

He bought the six eggs, five bananas, four apples, three oranges for the baby, two doughnuts and a packet of crisps for his tea.

But when he came out of the shop there was a bear.

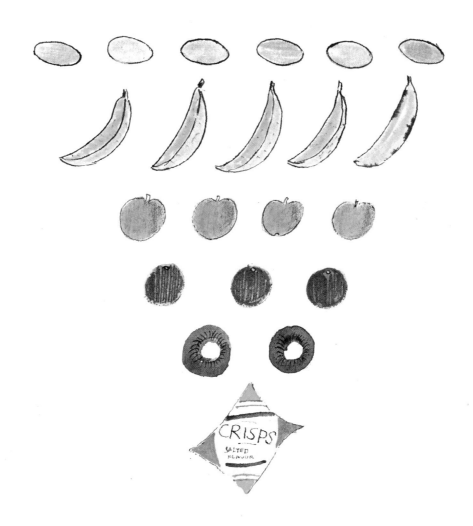

"I want those eggs," said the bear, "and if you
don't give them to me I will hug all the breath out
of you."

"If I threw an egg up in the air," said Steven,
"you are so slow I bet you couldn't even catch it."

"Me slow!" said the bear…

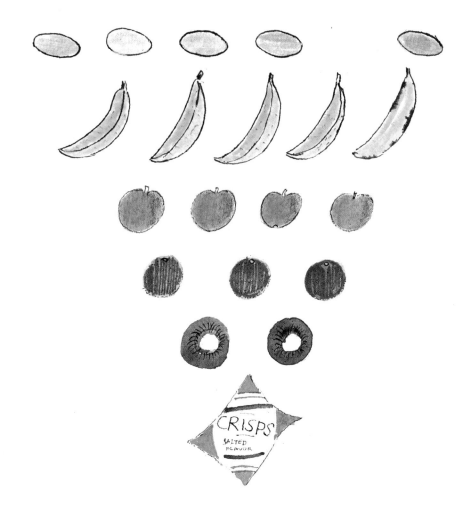

And Steven hurried on home carrying his basket.
But when he got to the house where the nasty
dog lived there was a monkey.

"Give me those bananas," said the monkey, "or I'll pull your hair."

"If I threw a banana on to that kennel, you're so noisy I bet you couldn't get it without waking the dog."

"Me noisy!" said the monkey…

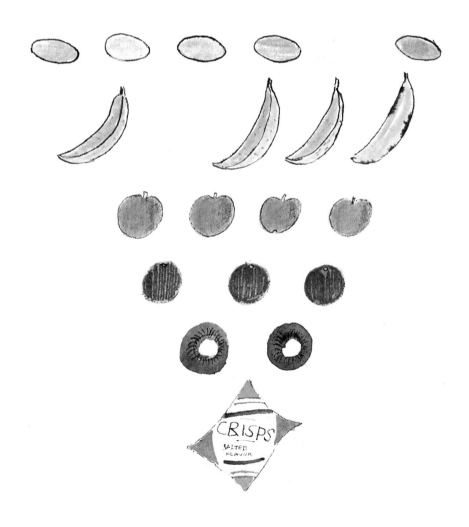

So Steven hurried on home carrying his basket.
But when he got to where the men were
digging up the pavement there was a kangaroo.

"Give me those apples you have in your basket," said the kangaroo, "or I'll thump you."

"If I threw an apple over that tent, you're so clumsy I bet you couldn't even jump over to get it."

"Me clumsy!" said the kangaroo…

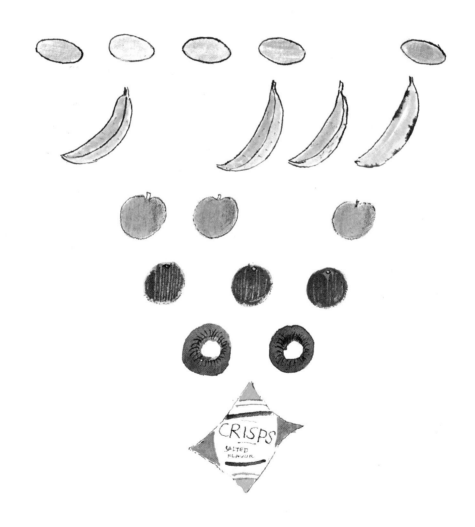

And Steven hurried on home carrying his basket.
    But when he got to the litter basket there was
a goat.

"Give me the oranges you have in your basket,"
said the goat, "or I'll butt you over the fence."
  "If I put an orange in that litter basket, you're so
stupid I bet you couldn't even get it out."
  "Me stupid!" said the goat…

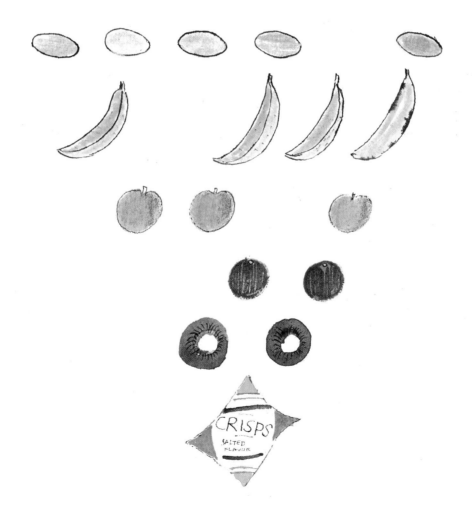

So Steven hurried on home carrying his basket.
   But when he got to the gap in the railings
there was a pig.

"Give me those doughnuts," said the pig, "or I'll squash you against the railings."

"If I put the doughnuts through that gap in the railings, you're so fat I bet you couldn't squeeze through and get them."

"Me fat!" said the pig…

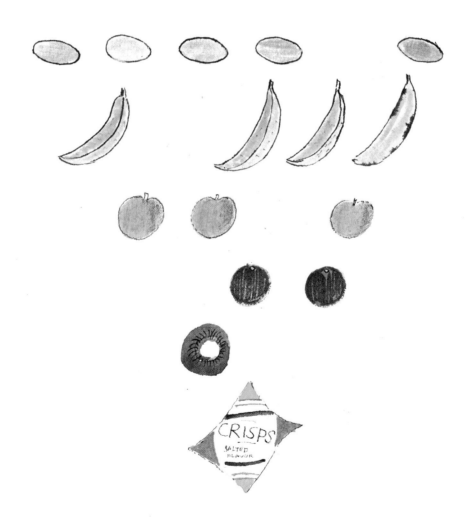

So Steven hurried on home carrying his basket.
   But when he got to number 25 there was
an elephant.

"Give me those crisps," said the elephant, "or I'll whack you with my trunk."

"If I put these crisps through that letter box, your trunk is so short I bet you could not even reach it."

"My trunk short!" said the elephant…

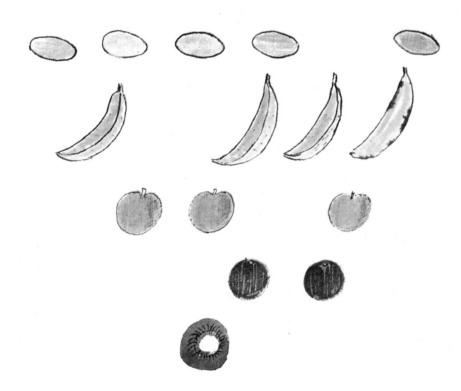

And Steven hurried on home carrying his basket.
    But when he got to his own house, there
was his mother.

"Where on earth have you been, Steven? I only asked you to get six eggs, five bananas, four apples, three oranges for the baby, two doughnuts and a packet of crisps. How could it have taken so long?"